MONSTER GOES TO SCHOOL

Virginia Mueller
pictures by Lynn Munsinger

Albert Whitman & Company, Morton Grove, Illinois

Other Books about Monster

A Halloween Mask for Monster
Monster and the Baby
Monster Can't Sleep
Monster's Birthday Hiccups
A Playhouse for Monster

Library of Congress Cataloging-in-Publication Data

Mueller, Virginia.
    Monster goes to school / Virginia Mueller :
pictures by Lynn Munsinger.
    p.   cm.
    Summary: At school Monster learns about time,
drawing a clock with pictures that represent his
day.
    ISBN 0-8075-5264-X (lib. bdg.)
    [1. Time—Fiction. 2. Clocks and watches—Fiction.
3. Monsters—Fiction.] I. Munsinger, Lynn, ill.
II. Title.
PZ7.M879Mr   1991
[E]—dc20   90-29873
                                                CIP
                                                 AC

Published in 1991 by Albert Whitman & Company,
Morton Grove, Illinois 60053-2723.
Published simultaneously in Canada by
General Publishing, Limited, Toronto.

To the National Coalition
for Campus Child Care. V.M.

To Samantha. L.M.

"It's time for school," Father said.

"I can tell time at school," Monster told Teacher.

"There is playtime,

storytime,

and music time.

There is lunchtime,

naptime,

and a time for drawing."

"Today I'll make something special," Monster said.
"What will you make?" Teacher asked.
"A school clock," Monster said.

Monster's clock did not
have numbers.

Monster's clock did not
have two hands.

Monster's clock did not
go tick-tock, tick tock.

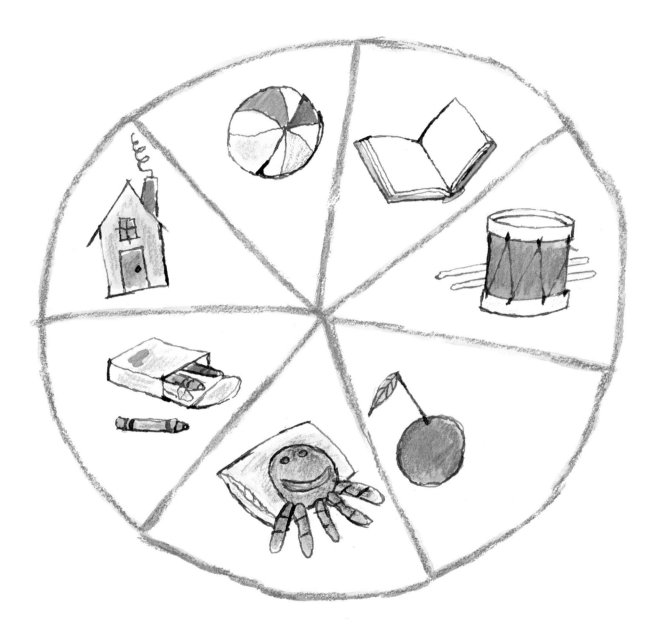

Monster's clock looked like this.

Monster asked, "Can you tell which picture is music time?"
"The drum!" said Teacher.
"And the apple is lunchtime," said Monster's friend.

When Mother came, Monster gave her his clock.

"This is my school clock," Monster said.

"I can tell time at school."

"What time is this?" Mother asked.

"Time to go home!" Monster said.